*For Dad, Steve, Ben, Randy and L̶ ̶ ̶ ̶ ̶ ̶.
Thank you to all of you who have supported us and provided us
with the time to make this happen.*

*We dedicate this book to all the black cats out there. We see you, for
you.*

Max the Cat

A BuchWyrm book
Published by BuchWyrm, LLC
341 Forest Cove Rd.
Anderson, South Carolina 29626
www.buchwyrm.com

ISBN– 13: 978-1-7358371-0-9

First Edition: September 2020
Printed in the United States of America

"Whenever I fall, I land on my feet.
How can they possibly think that of me?"

Then Max felt sad.
Perhaps they were right.

If he wasn't so unlucky,
he wouldn't be alone at night.

His colorful cat friends all got to sleep inside on warm cozy chairs.

Max slept outside under old porch stairs.

Max decided if he wanted a real home,
then he needed to change so he could belong.

He must discover a way to change his color.
Then he could be just like all the others!

The little lady that lives out near the dell,
I hear she brews potions
and can even cast spells!

The little lady gave Max a warning.
"You might not like what you see in the morning."

The little lady sighed
and opened the potion.
She poured it on Max's fur
in a swift steady motion.

He looked down at his paws in surprise.
He was covered in spots
of every color, shape, and size!

The people no longer ran in fear,
but their laughter
brought him many more tears.

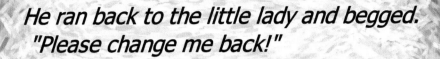
He ran back to the little lady and begged.
"Please change me back!"

For a limited time, fans can get a FREE
set of Max the Cat coloring pages.

Visit here for your free gift:

https://www.subscribepage.com/z7q8h0

Visit our website and

Enter to Win a Free Book or T-shirt!

www.buchwyrm.com

One Winner Every Month!

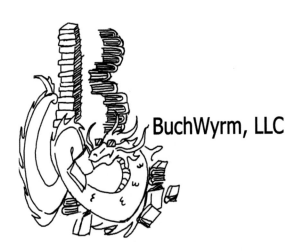

BuchWyrm, LLC

Made in the USA
Middletown, DE
09 November 2021